Jen McInnes

STEPPING
STONES

By Lucy Knisley

For
Taylor
&
Chelsea

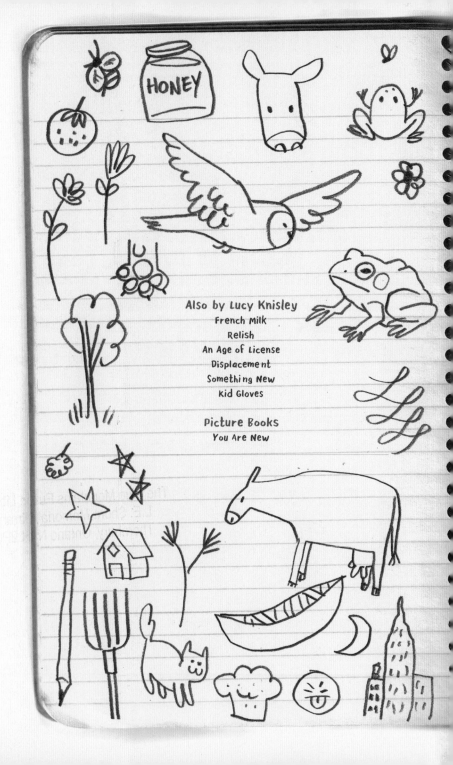

Also by Lucy Knisley
French Milk
Relish
An Age of License
Displacement
Something New
Kid Gloves

Picture Books
You Are New

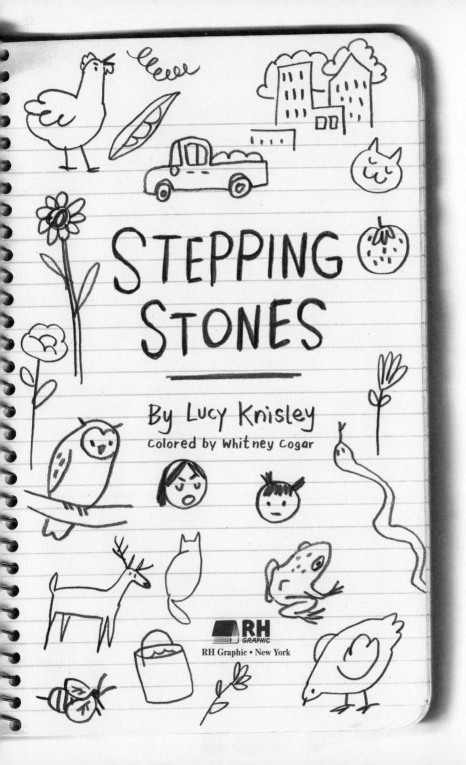

STEPPING STONES

By Lucy Knisley

colored by Whitney Cogar

RH Graphic • New York

Text, cover art, and interior art copyright © 2020 by Lucy Knisley
All rights reserved. Published in the United States by RH Graphic, an imprint of Random House Children's Books, a division of Penguin Random House LLC, New York.

RH Graphic with the book design is a trademark of Penguin Random House LLC.

Visit us on the Web! RHKidsGraphic.com • @RHKidsGraphic

Educators and librarians, for a variety of teaching tools, visit us at RHTeachersLibrarians.com

Library of Congress Cataloging-in-Publication Data
Names: Knisley, Lucy, author, artist. Title: Stepping stones / Lucy Knisley.
Description: First edition. | New York : RH Graphic, [2020] | Audience: Ages 8–12 | Audience: Grades 4–6 |
Summary: "Jen moves out to the country and has to put up with her mom and her mom's new boyfriend, as well as his kids. Suddenly part of a larger family in a new place, Jen isn't sure there is a place for her in this different world"—Provided by publisher.
Identifiers: LCCN 2019026160 | ISBN 978-1-9848-9684-1 (paperback) | ISBN 978-0-593-12524-3 (hardcover)
| ISBN 978-1-9848-9685-8 (library binding) | ISBN 978-1-9848-9686-5 (ebook)
Subjects: LCSH: Graphic novels. | CYAC: Graphic novels. | Families—Fiction. | Country life—Fiction.
Classification: LCC PZ7.7.K663 St 2020 | DDC 741.5/973—dc23

Designed by Patrick Crotty
Colored by Whitney Cogar

MANUFACTURED IN CHINA
10 9 8 7 6 5 4 3 2 1
First Edition

A comic on every bookshelf.

Stepping Stones was drawn with
Blackwing *602* pencils on bristol and
colored digitally.

Chapter
One

Hey, give me a hand with this.

Fine.

This is the chickens' water trough.

PAT PAT

The water fills up here, and the chickens drink from here. Cool, huh?

I guess.

Mom...

We're not gonna be... *eating* the chickens, are we?

Not at first. They'll start making eggs in a few months, and then we'll see how it goes.

I won't eat them.

You eat chicken!

But I didn't KNOW those chickens!

Where did you think those chickens come from? A place like this.

I'm still not eating them.

Hey, you two!

Bring that on over here!

Wow, honey, this is coming along great!

Thanks! You can put that over there.

Hey, Jen, you should help decide where this goes. You'll be bringing the chickens water every morning.

I will?

And giving them food, and cleaning the coop, and bringing the eggs in.

NOD

All of that? Every day? ALONE?

Well, on the weekends you'll have my girls to help you out. You'll love it! This beautiful place, good hard work!

I didn't even WANT chickens! Aren't we already doing enough farm stuff?

Come on! It'll be fun. You'll love the chickens.

I know you'll all be great little farmhands in no time!

Jen, why don't you take that bucket up to the barn and fill it with water for the trough.

Fine.

9

Map of Peapod Farm

Barn

House

Water Spout

me

(Future) Chicken Coop

Mom's garden

Pond

Mean goose

Woods

Hey, what are you doing way up here?

mew!

Huh, this ladder must go up to the hayloft.

Cool!

Secret hideout!

Chapter
Two

21

URGH!

Mom?

Aaaargh!

Hey, Mom, what's going on?

Those darn deer got into the garden again and ate all my lettuces!

What?

How?

Six-foot-tall fence

They're monsters! Last week it was my carrots! Why didn't anyone warn me about the deer up here?

25

These had better
be good eggs.

RING

Hello, um, Peapod Farm.

Hello, yes, this is the post office calling. Your delivery is ready for pickup.

We need to come to the post office?

Doesn't the mail usually get delivered?

Yep, this is a special kind of package.

Here, listen.

PEEP PEEP PEEP PEEP PEEP PEEP PEEP PEEP PEEP PEEP PEEP PEEP

MOM, THE CHICKENS ARE HERE!

What?

They're here?

They're on the phone! Check it out!

PEEP PEEP PEEP

Haha! Thank you!

We'll be right in!

They just come in the mail?!

I guess so! I ordered them from a catalog.

Hey, Mom, do you think they sent flightless birds "AIR MAIL"?

HA HA HA

POOP

WIPE

Okay, kiddo, you hop in the back and make sure they're okay.

I get to ride in the back of the truck?

Yep, just be careful back there.

33

Phew!

CRASH SPLASH PEEP PEEP PEEP

JENNY! Come help your mom get the berries in the truck!

I'm coming!

Are you excited about market? Your first real job!

What about when I worked for Dad at his office?

That doesn't count— you were inside all day!

Wait, do we need two blackboards for the stand?

Okay, Jen, I'm gonna run over to talk to the owner of Hillcroft Farms next door.

You're in charge till I get back, okay?

Wait, alone?

PEAPOD FARM

BERRIES-$7
GRANOLA-$8
RHUBARB-$5
FLOWERS-$6
ASPARAGUS-$5

Hello! I'll take three pints of goldenberries. Do you have change for a fifty?

uh...

uh, yes, um, here you go, uh...

EXCUSE ME. I'LL BE RIGHT BACK!

Uh...

ZOO

PEAPOD FARM
BERRIES—$7
GRANOLA—$8
RHUBARB—$5
FLOWERS—$6
ASPARAGUS—$5
/LB

I can't be here all the time, Jen, and Walter has to work at the farm.

I know, I know...

I know.

keep at it, okay? I know you'll get it.

RING
RING
RING
RING

Hi, you've reached Sam MacInnes. I'm in Toronto on business, so please contact my office if you need to speak with me. Thanks. BEEP!

oh yeah.

CLICK

Chapter
Three

Jen, this is Andrea and Reese.

Andrea and Reese, this is Jen.

I prefer Andy, if you please.

Okay.

Hi.

SCRITCH

Uh, do you wanna see some baby chicks?

Sure.

You girls have fun!

And don't forget to give the chickens some fresh water.

I prefer Jen, too.

what?

Walter called me Jenny. I've told him before that I don't really like that.

Well, my dad was just being nice.

oh.

okay.

Here are the chicks. They're about four weeks old now.

How many are girls and how many are boys?

Um.

I'm not sure.

I think this one's a boy!

I'll name him Claude!

And that one's Pierre, and that one's Maurice, and that one's Jean-Luc.

Well, hopefully some of them are girls, that way they'll start laying eggs in like six weeks.

Not Claude.

Right, Claude?

Okay, this one can be Chiquita. Get it?

No, that doesn't fit with the French theme!

Here's where the feed is.

Why is it in a garbage can?

Mom says it's to keep the raccoons out.

Gross. I'd keep it INSIDE the henhouse, so the raccoons couldn't get into it at all.

That's a pretty good idea.

I get straight As. What are your grades?

Girls! Time to head into town for market!

We gotta go.

Okay, hop in.

Into the back? Isn't that unsafe?

Well, I guess...

But I like it back here! It's fun!

You can ride back there, but I'm riding up front with a seatbelt. I hope we don't get into an ACCIDENT.

Andy's right. We should all be up front. Let's go.

But it's so crowded up there!

Right now, young ladies, or we're going to be late for market!

Good luck, girls!

Okay, Jen, why don't you give Andy the rundown.

I've got to go speak to the market manager about our fee. I'll be back in a bit.

Peapod Farm
Berries .$7
Flowers $4

Okay, um, the flowers are four dollars a bunch. The berries are seven a box.

We have to put the berries in the bag carefully, or we'll squish them.

Why don't you just give them the box, to keep the berries safe?

We could, but then we'd run out of boxes.

Mom says not to, unless they ask.

Hm.

Fine, but that's not how I'd do it.

Mom's granola is eight dollars.

Eight? That's a lot for a bag of cereal.

She makes it herself.

We should do a special sale! Buy a box of berries and get granola twenty-five percent off.

Uh...

What's twenty-five percent of eight?

What? That's like a basic fraction.

Here, let me.

Here you are, enjoy your purchases.

Andy, maybe you'd like to handle the cash box, since you're so good with numbers.

Jen, why don't you tidy up the sign a bit?

Of course!

I'll get this organized. I'm gonna be an engineer when I grow up!

Come to Peapod Farm for a special on granola!

Peapod Farm

Peapod Farm
BERRIES — $7
GRANOLA — $8
RHUBARB — $4
FLOWERS — $4
SPECIAL: BUY A
BOX OF BERRIES &
GET 25% OFF OF
HOMEMADE GRANOLA

DUMP

SPECIAL

DING DONG DONG

That's three PM!
Time to pack up.

Good work today.

Thanks, Mom.

You've earned this.

Why don't you two go check out the market for a bit?

What are you gonna do with yours?

I dunno. There's no movie theaters or comic shops in town...

I'm going to SAVE mine. For COLLEGE.

That's smart.

Yep. I'm gonna go to a great college and get a good job when I grow up.

But you can go ahead and spend yours if you'd like.

Hello there. What do you think of my bees?

They're so cool!

You work at a stand, too, right?

Yep. Over there.

You guys had a special today, didn't you?

Yeah.

Well I've got a special, too. A free honey stick to a fellow farmer!

Thanks!

Okay, we're all packed up. Hop in, everybody.

Chapter
Four

next weekend

Hey, what are you doing?

LEAP

There was a big bullfrog! I think there are lots of them. I hear them croaking at night!

My dad says that noise is the toads— are you sure you didn't see a toad?

BLIP

I see it!

What?

The frog?

I wonder if I could catch it!

Oh, we could make a little house for it!

I think I can sneak up on it.

You're going in there?

MOM!

She's in the shower.

What's up?

Andy let my frog get away!

It wasn't YOUR frog!

IT WAS, TOO! I CAUGHT IT!

I did, too!

And I NAMED him!

SHE WAS A GIRL!

okay, calm down.

Jenny, you've gotten used to being the only kid around here. You've got to learn to share and take turns.

But...

But...

You can't just rule the roost. I know you're not used to siblings, but you've got to learn.

URGH

Okay, Miss Drama Queen!

Hi, sweetie. You okay?

Fine.

I know, it's a lot to get used to with the move and the girls spending the weekends here.

Yeah.

There are gonna be a lot of bumps along the way, but we'll all get through it. You just have to be a good hostess.

What?

These girls are away from their mom. This farm is new to them, too. We need to be gracious and try to share our things with them.

But she's such a mean, bossy know-it-all!

That's not nice, Jen.

She makes me feel stupid!

And she took my frog.

Couldn't you have shared the frog?

So she gets to decide everything?

What to name it and where to put it and how to run market?

Sweetie, she's away from home.

SO AM I!

This is our home now.

It's not mine. I didn't choose to be here.

I want to go back to the city.

To Dad.

Well, that's not an option anymore. We're here now, and we have to make the best of it.

I don't have to make the best out of anything!

You don't get to tell me how to feel about this.

Chapter
Five

Next Weekend

Hi, girls! How was market this week?

Great!

I introduced some new sales techniques into our business, and people seemed to like it a lot!

Jen dropped a whole bag of granola and spilled it.

I couldn't help it! I was trying to help like five customers!

Maybe if you got a little more organized, you could handle it.

You already can't even handle working the cash box.

What? Jenny, is that true?

She has trouble with the math.

You know, sweetie, you really should work on that. You ought to be able to make change if you're going to work the market.

RUSTLE
RUSTLE

RUSTLE
RUSTLE

My sister is having a tantrum. Just like everyone today, I guess.

WAHH

I miss my mommyyyyy!

SNUFF

I hate it here! I hate it!

It's scary and we have to be outside all the time and I want to go hoooome!

She does this sometimes.

Crybaby.

WAHH!

PLOP

okay, honey, why don't you lie down for a little bit and try to calm down.

I'll be right downstairs.

SNIFF

Hey, Reese, you okay?

I get it.

I'm not crazy about this place, either.

Really?

But you're like... a farmer.

You wanna hear a funny story about when I first moved here?

Sure.

I went down to the pond to see if there were any turtles there.

There were geese nesting at the side of the pond. I didn't know geese were so...mean.

They made this horrible hissing sound, trying to scare me away from their nest.

I tried to climb a tree to get away from them...

...but I didn't know the tree had a hornet's nest in it.

I got stung on the eye! I fell out of the tree into a big mud puddle!

There's so much there! Art and stores and music on the streets.

The hot dog carts. The way the lights look at night...

That stuff is okay, but it's also smelly and crowded. And you can never go anywhere alone outside.

And it's loud! Mommy says it's called the city that never sleeps for a reason!

It's pretty loud here, too! The frogs make noise all night!

Ribbit, ribbit ribbit, wake up!

Haha!

That's true!

How's everybody doing in here?

It's been a rough day.

So I thought I'd make some...

...before-dinner brownies!

Maybe it'll be a vanilla goat!

Or a strawberry goat!

How about a root beer goat!

Yum!

Ha!

You drew that without tracing?

Yeah.

Jen is very good.

In Fact...

I've been thinking— you should draw the labels for my granola.

I think it would really help sales to have a nice drawing on the bags.

Really?

Yeah! You could draw a special logo for the farm!

Like a goat! Or a peapod, I guess.

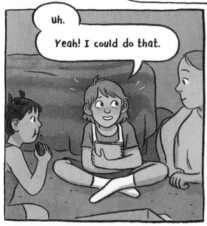

uh.

Yeah! I could do that.

Thanks, kiddo.

You're a big help.

RUFFLE

I'm not much help at market.

That's not true.

Pea
Pod
FARM

Chapter
Six

Next weekend

Ya don't just wanna yank on it.

You gotta be gentle.

You take your thumb and forefinger and wrap 'em around the top of the teat.

Then you close your fist toward your palm, like so.

So! Who wants to go first?

Okay, then, step right up.

Cool!

I wanna try!

Thanks for showing the girls the ropes, Steve.

No problem, Walt. It's what neighbors do.

You wanna give it a try, Reese?

Now you skim the cream off the top, just like this.

Next part's the most fun.

You just shake it.

That's it?

NOD

Yep! That's all there is to it.

SHAKE SHAKE SHAKE

Thanks again, Steve. Mike.

Anytime, neighbor. Our nephew's about their age. He's coming to stay with us in a couple of weeks. You should bring the girls by to meet him.

Okay, girls, let's get home. We've got a big project ahead of us.

Do you think that cow would eat her own butter?

Ew!

I hope you kids are all...

Buttered up!

UGH.

Because today you'll be laying paths!

But there already are paths.

Yes, but when it rains, Miss Smarty Pants, they get muddy. We need to keep the paths dry by laying wood chips down.

POND

BARN

MOM'S GARDEN

HOUSE

PATH

WOOD PILE

CHICKEN COOP

That way we can get all around the farm and woods easily with the wheelbarrow.

SIGH.

Oh, and one more thing.

Watch out for rattlesnakes.

Mr. Fisher was telling me there are a few of them back there in the woods, so be careful.

Okay, have fun!

Why do you think your dad said that?

About the snakes?

Yeah.

Who knows. He's funny like that.

I don't think it's funny.

You just don't understand his humor.

I guess not.

He used to be a lawyer. He's very smart.

Okay.

But I guess... he shouldn't joke about snakes. Maybe he doesn't know how scared you are.

Do you think your dad and my mom will get married?

I don't know.

It would be weird, I guess.

Yeah. Pretty weird.

But also it would be cool to have sisters.

It's been kinda... nice to have some kids around when you and Reese come for weekends.

Sisters are overrated.

You have to share everything with them, and you fight a lot.

But I like coming to visit, too.

I guess we'd be stepsisters, but the only stepsisters I know are the ones from *Cinderella*.

Haha! Yeah! The evil ones!

Shovel those wood chips, Cinderandy! Clean the chicken coop, Cinderjen!

Ha!

Whoa!

Look out!

Huh?

ZOOM

Oh no.

Reese!

146

147

148

Chapter
Seven

next weekend

SNIP

Are the chickens supposed to be in here?

Yes!

They're helping by eating the bad bugs that try to eat the flowers and veggies.

Oh, I thought the fence was supposed to keep them out.

It's supposed to keep the deer out, but every time I think I fix it, they seem to find a way in.

At least there are enough flowers left for market!

They didn't *all* get eaten!

How's the granola label project coming?

Good!

Almost done.

I get to come to market this week, too!

uh-huh.

I'm gonna be the flower girl!

That's for a wedding, not market, silly.

You heard the lady.

Last one in is a rotten egg.

I expect big sales today, girls! Lots of city people up for the holiday weekend.

I have to work my rotation at the board's table today, so you girls are in charge of the stand.

Well done, Reese!

Excuse me.

Peapod Farm

I just wanted to say how nice it is to see you three sisters working together here at market.

My sisters and I used to work at our dad's shop when we were kids.

You three take care of each other, okay?

Okay!

Thanks.

I...

The signs are my job.

Oh, come on.

You're not the only one who can write on a chalkboard.

Honestly, Jenny, if you worked a little harder in math, you could work the till with Andy.

Then you could *really* be a help to your mom here at market.

Hey, where are you girls going?

Hey! We still need to pack up!

Jen!

wait up.

I'm sorry—my dad was being kind of a jerkface.

I don't know why he hates me so much.

He doesn't. He's like that with everybody. You just gotta let it go, or he'll argue until he wins, even if he isn't right.

FARMERS MARKET

Chapter
Eight

next weekend

CRICK

SIZZLE

welp, that was a pretty good egg.

The best egg!

okay, let's head to market! Dishes in the sink!

What's that fishing wire doing there? Were you fishing this morning, Dad?

Nope. That was for a special project.

A fishing project?

No, it was meant to be a surprise...

I read that if you run some fishing twine in the woods around the farm, it'll keep the deer away.

Curses.

Foiled!

They don't like the feel of trying to cross it, so they stay out of the farm and leave Jessica's garden alone.

Oh!

I spent the morning putting twine up to keep your garden from getting chomped.

Thank you!

It broke my heart to see you fighting a losing battle against the local fauna.

Maybe now I can try lettuce again!

Mmm, lettuce! Do they make pizza plants?

Daddy! That's silly!

Hello there!

Oh, hello, Mr. Fisher. Can I interest you in our special today?

Haha, thanks, but your parents give me plenty already!

You lot are good neighbors to have around!

I just wanted to introduce you to our nephew, Eddie.

He comes to help us with the harvest.

TUG

Thought you girls might like to know another farm kid in our little neck of the woods.

Hi.

Hello!

Hi.

Hi!

Would you care to try a sample of our delicious granola?

Uh

okay.

So are you all, um...sisters?

Um

Well...

Err

Stepsisters, basically.

But we're not evil!

Sort of, part-time sisters.

Okay.

Walt says you girls spotted a rattler in the woods behind the farm a couple of weeks ago!

It was as long as me! And it had huge fangs!

We barely made it out alive!

We're not going back there anytime soon, that's for sure.

No way!

Well, glad you're all okay! Nice to see you girls!

Nice to meet you! See you around.

Yes!

See you! And you, too! I mean, nice to...

Smooth.

Ugh, let's just forget that happened.

Hot one, eh, girls?

Sure is, Mr. Archer!

I thought our beeswax was going to melt out here! But at least the sales were good.

You three look like melty candles!

Here you go, a few honey sticks before you melt!

You three are a good team. You ever want some extra work, come and help out at the hives.

Thanks!

Thank you!

Honey!

DING DONG

There's the bell! We can all go home and cool off!

Yay!

we have to winterize the chicken coop, and plow the summer crops to make way for winter ones, and we told the neighbors we'd help with their pumpkin patch.

SIGH

But we don't have to do any of that today, do we?

THUD
THUD

We could tell secrets here, and nobody could hear us!

It's like a secret cave.

A Note From The Author

When I was a kid, my parents split up and my mom and I moved from New York City to a little farm in the country.

She wanted to grow flowers and berries and get her hands dirty. I wanted to read comic books INSIDE where it was CLEAN, but sometimes when you're a kid, you're just along for the ride.

Mom

Me

I wasn't always thrilled with my mom's decision to become a super farmer lady, but I didn't have much of a choice about becoming a not-so-super farm kid.

Then my mom got a boyfriend. He was loud, bossy, and annoying. I'd never met such an annoying grown-up! And his daughters! A loud, bossy kid and her whiny little sister! Suddenly, I was sharing my room every weekend with these total strangers.

One of the worst things about being a kid is finding yourself in these situations where you have no control over the decisions the adults are making that affect you. But sometimes it's also one of the best things— to find yourself in a situation you couldn't possibly have chosen for yourself, totally at sea. It can sometimes bring unexpected beauty, and introduce strangers that become family.

My "Andy" is still loud and bossy, but she's also brilliant and funny. My "Reese" is much less whiney now, and much cooler than all of us, as she has always been.

My "Walter" was both annoying and beloved until his dying day.

My mom is still getting her hands dirty and loving her life in the country, and I am so thankful to her for forcing me to endure such a beautiful childhood full of rattlesnakes and ponds and lots more stories to tell.

(Another little note)

Big Shocker: I am bad at math.

$$\begin{array}{r} 4 \\ \times 7 \\ \hline 28 \end{array}$$

I'm not just BAD at math, though;
I'm dyscalculiac! It's a little like
dyslexia, but rather than reading, this one
impairs your ability to process numbers
and magnitude.

When I graduated, I breathed a sigh of
relief that I'd never have to do math
again, but then I became a comic artist
and had to learn how to measure and
divide a page of panels! It was like
algebra RETURNING FROM THE GRAVE TO
HAUNT ME. IM BACK!

Being "good" at something is less
important than trying or practicing. After
all, I became a comic artist after years
and YEARS of practicing my drawing and
writing. And I'm much better at math than
I used to be! My "Andy," of course, is an
engineer, and sometimes she has to draw
diagrams and she's rotten at it, but she's
getting better, too. Who'da thunk it?

Acknowledgments:

Thank you to Taylor, Chelsea, and Georgia.
Thank you to the Rhinebeck Farmers' Market.
Thank you to my fellow children of divorce.

Thank you to my publishing team at Random
House Graphic! Gina Gagliano and
Whitney Leopard and Patrick Crotty!
Thank you to Whitney Coger
for beautiful colors.
Thank you to Holly Bemiss
for being my champion.

Thank you to bees for your honey and
gardens for your flowers and bushes for
your berries and cows for your milk and
barns for your kittens.

Thank you to Warren, who I miss and who
would have been very sweet and very
annoying about this whole book.

Thank you to John and Pal,
who are my faves.

Author shown with pencil stubs used during the making of this book!

About The Author

Lucy Knisley grew up with one foot in New York City and the other on an upstate farm.

An only child with divorced parents, she was an avid comic book and fantasy reader, who began to navigate the unfamiliar world of step-familial melodrama when she was eleven.

She graduated from the School of the Art Institute of Chicago, followed by the Center for Cartoon Studies, and began publishing graphic novels (a travelogue) at the age of twenty-two.

She has always tried to use her work to make people feel less alone through her honest and confessional comics. Her topics range from travel, adulthood, ailing grandparents, foreign romance, wedding planning, food, and reproductive health.

She lives in Chicago, where she likes riding her bike with her son and partner, and reading fantasy novels and comic books.

LucyKnisley.com

RH GRAPHIC

THE SUMMER 2020 LIST

CRABAPPLE TROUBLE
By Kaeti Vandorn

Life isn't easy when you're an apple.

Callaway and Thistle must figure out how to work together—with delicious and magical results.

Young Chapter Book

KERRY AND THE KNIGHT OF THE FOREST
By Andi Watson

Kerry needs to get home!

To get back to his parents, Kerry gets lost in a shortcut. He will have to make tough choices and figure out who to trust—or remain lost in the forest . . . forever.

Middle-Grade

STEPPING STONES
By Lucy Knisley

Jen did not want to leave the city.

She did not want to move to a farm.

And Jen definitely did not want to get two new "sisters."

Middle-Grade

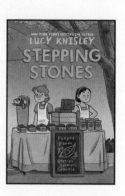

SUNCATCHER
By Jose Pimienta

Beatriz loves music—more than her school, more than her friends—and she won't let anything stop her from achieving her dreams.

Even if it means losing everything else.

Young Adult

FIND US ONLINE AT @RHKIDSGRAPHIC AND RHKIDSGRAPHIC.COM